Five Polar Bears

By Wes Nehring

Illustrated by Alek Eglinton

Five polar bears went out to play,
it's gonna be a good day!

Five little polar bears playing in the light,
one says, "I'm gonna lay here til night."

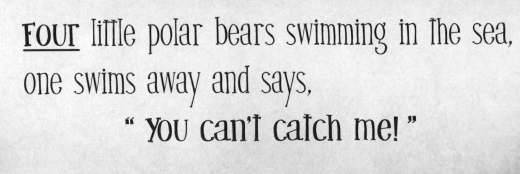

FOUR little polar bears swimming in the sea,
one swims away and says,
" YOU can't catch me! "

Three polar bears went out to play,
it's gonna be a good day!

Three little polar bears looking for a meal,
one says, " I'll go look for a seal! "

TWO little polar bears playing real nice,
one jumps up and falls through the ice!

one polar bear went out to play,
it's gonna be a good day!

Polar bear polar bear now you're the only one!
Are you the only bear who had too much fun?

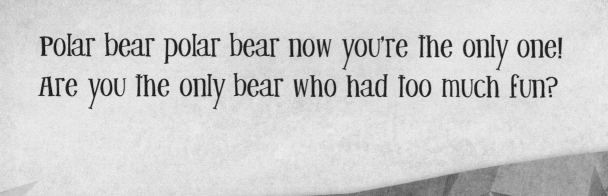

And you say, " yes oh yes I'm tired of playing games.
So I'm gonna go back home and fall asleep inside my...

...cave. "   Goodnight polar bear!

The End.

About the Author: Wes Nehring

Wes Nehring graduated from the University of Wisconsin Stout in 2009 with a B.S. in Early Childhood Education. He currently resides in Menomonie, WI with his bride Caitlin and two little children. Together they enjoy gardening, cooking, and the daily gift of life & family.

About the Illustrator: Alek Eglinton

Alek Eglinton graduated from the University of Wisconsin Stout in 2013 with a B.F.A. in Industrial Design. He currently lives in Dubuque, IA where he designs furniture and spends time with friends and family. Alek enjoys designing, reading, and traveling.

Dedicated to Jesus, the author of the greatest story ever told.
- John 14:6

Lindsay Cibos polar bear sketches were used to make *5 Polar Bears* a reality. Special thanks to Lindsay see her talented work at the website: http://www.jaredandlindsay.com/

Picture of the Nehrings courtesy of 1,000 Words Photography by Nicky Wilke.

Picture of Alek taken by Adrianna Joy of A&J Photography.

Jason Kadinger remastered the song which goes with the book.

For the free song download which goes with the book and other information regarding *5 Polar Bears* please visit:

www.mrwesmusic.com

Made in the USA
Charleston, SC
18 February 2016